THE GENIE IN THE JAR

The Genie in the Jar

NIKKI GIOVANNI

ILLUSTRATED BY CHRIS RASCHKA

HENRY HOLT AND COMPANY   NEW YORK

for Nina Simone

—N.G.

for Ingo

—C.R.

Henry Holt and Company, LLC, *Publishers since 1866*
175 Fifth Avenue, New York, New York 10010
www.HenryHoltKids.com
Henry Holt® is a registered trademark of Henry Holt and Company, LLC.
Text copyright © 1996 by Nikki Giovanni
Illustrations copyright © 1996 by Chris Raschka
Distributed in Canada by H. B. Fenn and Company Ltd.

Library of Congress Cataloging-in-Publication Data
Giovanni, Nikki.
The genie in the jar / by Nikki Giovanni;
illustrated by Chris Raschka.
Summary: In this hymn to the power of art and of love,
the words create images of black songs and black looms, inspiring
readers to trust their hearts.
1. Afro-Americans—Juvenile poetry.   2. Children's poetry, American.
[1. Afro-Americans—Poetry.   2. American poetry.]
I. Raschka, Christopher, ill.   II. Title.
PS3557.I55G46   1996   811'.54—dc20   95-23503

ISBN-13: 978-0-8050-6076-8 / ISBN-10: 0-8050-6076-6
First paperback edition—1998
First published in hardcover in 1996 by Henry Holt and Company
Printed in China on acid-free paper. ∞
10 9 8 7 6 5 4

The artist used India ink, oil sticks, and watercolor
on Fabriano Ingres paper to create the illustrations for this book.

and spin it around

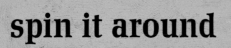

spin it around

don't

prick your finger

take a note

and spin it around

on the Black loom

on the Black loom

careful baby

don't prick your finger

take the air

and weave the sky

around the Black loom

around the Black loom

make the sky sing a Black song
sing a blue song

sing my song make the sky
sing a Black song

from the Black loom from the Black loom

careful baby

don't prick your finger

take a genie

and put her in a jar

put her in a jar
wrap the sky around her

take the genie and put her in a jar
wrap the sky around her

listen to her sing
sing a Black song our Black song
from the Black loom

singing to me
from the Black loom

careful baby

don't prick your finger